A Detective's Determination

By: Acai L.K. Arop

"Be yourself. Live your dreams. Love your body. Be able to say no and mean it. And most importantly, believe in yourself."

Dedications:

- First and foremost I would like to dedicate this book to my daughter Alek and my son Mathiang, I love you guys with all my heart and soul forever.

- I dedicate this book to my uncle Kizito Arop who was my best friend who believed in me, Rest in Peace dearest uncle, I will always love you very much and forever.

- I also would like to dedicate this book Especially to my father Louis Kuol Arop, who taught me right from wrong and would give me advice when I would ask and need his advice. Love you always Daddy forever...

- To my family, love you all very much...

- To my very special friends that believed in me and tell me Never To Give Up on writing until the book is completed and finished. PS. You know who are. Love you guys...

- I would like to especially dedicate this book to my best friend and cousin Nyanjok Ngong and my cousin Biong Ring Deng Biong who have passed away, you are forever in our hearts and will be remembered always. We love you and never forget..

- I dedicate this book to my best Friend James Wek Amoul Dau, who suddenly had passed away, he'll be missed and forever in my heart. We Love you...

- I am here to dedicate my book to a member of the Sudanese Community and an uncle Thomas Makuoi who had suddenly passed away our hearts are surely broken and he will surely be missed and never forgotten.

- To the Females that were told that you won't amount to nothing, Chose something that would make you happy from the **Inside and Never Give Up on it No Matter the Circumstances Whatsoever!!!**

"Strength does not come
from winning
Your Struggles develops
your strength
When you go through
hardships and decide not
to surrender, that is
True Strength."

Chapter 1

Ayana stared down at the streets of Richmond, the sun casting a warm glow over the streets filled with afternoon shoppers. But her mind wasn't on the shoppers, but on the many cases - past and present - that she knew so intimately. Rarely did she have a moment where she wasn't focused on her work but she didn't mind. This was her life, the one she'd worked so hard for.

Throughout her work as a detective for Richmond's police department, one question has always haunted her.

Why do people do such horrible things to those who seem so undeserving? Why commit crimes that have such a negative impact on every level of society - beginning with Richmond PD? It made no sense to her.

As she scribbled down some notes over the last few cases she'd yet to report on, the phone rang.

"Hello," she said. "This is Detective Harris. How may I help you?"

"Detective Harris." It was Chief Thomas Hernandez. His confident assertiveness carried through the phone and made her sit straighter. "Jonathan Evans is coming to see you soon."

"Jonathan Evans?"

"The new Assistant Chief of Police."

"Oh. Thanks for letting me know, Chief."

When the call ended, Ayana returned to her work but she couldn't stop thinking about what the Chief had said. Why would the Assistant Chief of Police be coming to see her? She might be an okay detective - all right, she was better than 'okay' - but still.

"Excuse me?" a voice came from above her desk.

She looked up from her case files and bolted to her feet. It was the Assistant Chief of Police. Hernandez could have told her he'd be there in two seconds! The Assistant Chief was surprisingly young and African-American. She herself was from the Sudan originally. Maybe he was, too. Not that she'd have much time for small talk.

"Good afternoon, Detective Harris," Evans said as he pulled a chair over from an empty desk and sat in front of her. His voice was low and strong. "My name is Jonathan Evans, Assistant Police Chief with the Virginia police department. I've been temporarily transferred to your department seeing as I need your help - and Richmond PD's help in general - on a case that must be solved as soon as possible."

He specifically wanted her help? Ayana leaned forward, intrigued. "How can I help, sir?"

"Detective Harris, this case is a difficult one and the suspect has proven difficult to catch as well. The suspect has violated several women in their own homes. We believe he follows each one for days until, one night, he strikes."

Evans handed her the file they had so far - it was thick, bulging with scraps of paper and photographs and transcriptions of the different women's testimonies. The case was a disturbing one, no doubt about it.

"May I ask why you wanted me, sir?"

"Look around you, Harris," he said. "How many female detectives do you see?"

None. That was how many. Richmond PD might be up-and-coming in some ways but many of the senior detectives and higher up execs hadn't gotten it through their head that a woman could do this job just as well as a man.

Sometimes even better.

"Because this case deals with women in a vulnerable situation, we felt it best to get a female detective on the case. And you ranked highest in your class. In all the classes, actually."

She looked away, didn't want to do anything stupid like blush.

"Plus," he added, leaning closer, "I went over your file myself. I think there's a lot of dedication and relentlessness trapped up there." He pointed at her forehead. "You've got what it takes."

"Thank you, sir."

After Evans left, she went through case file bit by bit and became increasingly angry as she did so.

Why? Who would a man like Andrew Wilks - that was the suspect's name - wake up one day and decide that his sole mission would be to terrorize women around the county?

She would find him. She vowed it to herself and to all the women of Virginia. She would find this Wilks and put him behind bars. Then perhaps she could find out what made him tick so that the same pattern wouldn't be repeated in other psychos.

There was always the chance of a simple psychological explanation. Had Wilks been rejected by a woman in his life and then decided to take out his hurt pride on other women? She'd have to check into that angle, see if Wilks had a former girlfriend or wife that could provide some hints to his whereabouts.

The next morning, after finishing the file, Ayana snapped it shut and left for Evans' office instead of calling him. She had a lot of thoughts and they would be better said in person instead of over the phone.

His office door was open and she knocked on it.

"Excuse me, Chief Evans. I'm sorry to interrupt, but I had to see you about this case." She waved the file for emphasis. "May I come in?"

"Of course." He rose and helped her to a chair.

Once she was seated, she took a deep breath. "Chief Evans, I'm here to let you know that I'd be happy to assist you with this case. I believe that Andrew Wilks needs to be apprehended and I believe that I'm the detective to find him."

Evans nodded. "Good. I'm glad we're on the same page."

"I have an idea for capturing him," Ayana said before she lost the courage to suggest what she'd come up with last night. She wanted to catch Wilks, no question about it, but her plan was risky at best. She could end up dead at worst. But wasn't this what she'd signed up for when taking the entrance exam to police academy?

"Oh?" Evans said.

"I want to go undercover. Live in his area, go to the places he frequents. Put myself out there. It's the only way we can draw him out into the open." He was already shaking his head 'no'. She had to convince him! "Chief Evans, I'm the best person to do this.

I won't let him get the drop on me and I'll be wired at all times. I can do this so he never hurts another woman again."

Evans still didn't look happy about this. "Tell me how you have this planned out, Harris," he said.

Okay. She took in a deep breath. She could do this. "The file indicates a few places Wilks has been seen at regularly, one bar in particular. I'd go to that bar when he normally would. I'd relax, at like a normal customer. When he comes into the bar, I'll strike up a conversation and get his interest. Once I know he's not going to bolt, I'll arrest him. Simple as that."

He studied her. "All right," he said. "It could work. But I will only allow it if you're wired at all times and if there are several plainclothesmen inside the bar, ready to help you if there's the smallest amount of trouble."

She nodded. "Sounds good to me, sir. I'll head home and get ready to go undercover tonight."

Ayana walked into the bar. It hadn't taken long to choose her outfit. A black skirt that brushed mid-thigh. A maroon blouse with a couple buttons opened at the top. Black, high-heeled boots. And her hair down, swishing against her back. She wanted to look good without being too provocative. This outfit would surely catch Wilks' eye.

She didn't make eye contact with any of the plainclothesmen but she knew they were there. Just as she knew the tiny earpiece was there, one reason she'd worn her hair long and loose.

The bar was smaller than many but she found a comfortable spot where she could watch the door for Wilks. She ordered a beer but didn't drink it.

The door opened.

Wilks!

He sat down at the bar and ordered a drink.

With one quick breath to steady her nerves, Ayana left her beer and joined Wilks at the bar. "Good evening," she said. "How are you?" She tried to inject some flirtiness into her tone, something like how a stranger hitting on a guy would sound.

"I'm good," Wilks said, grinning at her. He hesitated the smallest moment before saying, "My name's Andrew Wilks."

"Nice to meet you. I'm Allison Jackson." Using a false name was essential in undercover work.

"So why're you here?"

She sighed. "Oh, I just come here to relax. Unwind from my job."

"Me too!" He grinned again. "Where do you work?"

Would now be a good time to reveal that she was a detective, here to arrest him? She thought not. "I'm, ah, a defense attorney," she said. "I've been thinking of going off on my own lately, though."

A bit of guilt twinged in her at the lie, even if it was necessary to catch a rapist.

"Let me guess...you're not even married, right?"

She stared at him. It was such a personal question from - he thought - a complete stranger. "Andrew, I'd rather not talk about it. I put myself into my work to make the world better."

Wilks was almost done his drink. She needed to act fast. But first, she had a question for him. "Andrew, may *I* ask a question now?"

When he nodded, she said, "What are you afraid of...and why?"

"Now, that's two questions."

She smiled. "But I'm hoping you'll answer them anyway. Please?"

"Well, I've never been asked questions like that, but let's see..." He thought for a moment, then said, "There's things I'm afraid of, things that might get in trouble one of these days. To tell you the truth, just between you and me, I'm afraid of getting my heart broken again. I loved a woman once but she broke my heart. Took everything from me."

This was more than she'd hoped for. "Andrew, why are you telling me this? We've never even met before?"

"I'm telling you because, well, because I feel like one of these days the police will find out what all I've done. And I want to have one person on my side in all of this."

He was making it so easy for her. The time had come.

"Andrew, my real name is Ayana Harris. I'm a detective for Richmond PD and I'm here to arrest you."

She snapped the cuffs on him when he was still in shock.

But when he came out of shock, he only asked, very politely, "How did you know that I was your suspect?"

Ayana didn't answer him. She didn't have her own thoughts together yet, was too busy processing all that had passed - and so quickly, too! The last thing she wanted to do was share her innermost feelings and thoughts with a serial rapist.

"I'll speak with you when we're back at the station," she finally said.

When they returned to the station, she'd interrogate him, get a confession from him, and then the investigation would be complete.

Chapter 2

Ayana walked into the interrogation room. She still had trouble believing that they - she - had apprehended Andrew Wilks so quickly and with so little trouble. Usually, cases dragged on for weeks or even months. But not this time. It was a small blessing in this world of grueling hours and discouraging developments.

Wilks sat in a chair, the table separating them.

He stared up at her, a mixture of amusement and defiance on his face.

"I want to know why you told me what you did," Ayana said, placing her hands on the table and leaning forward. "I was a complete stranger to you and yet you trusted me with sensitive, personal information. I want to know why."

He smirked up at her. "Feelin' guilty about lying to me?"

"No," she snapped. But he was closer than he knew.

"You want to know what exactly was going through my mind and why I did such awful things to the women I dated," Wilks said. "I apologize for hurtin' them."

She didn't trust him for a moment.

"You're going away for a long time, Wilks. Life, if we're lucky. Now that you've confessed - and I do have all that on tape," she added, waving to the recorder on the table, "you'll be jailed, brought to trial, and tried for your crimes."

She looked back through the two-way mirror and nodded.

A couple seconds later, the door opened and two guards came in for Wilks.

"Put your hands behind your back," Ayana said. "These guards will escort you to your cell."

She watched, hands fisted on her hips, as the guards led Wilks away.

One rapist down, about a thousand more to go. But she couldn't deny the small sense of satisfaction that came from putting another criminal where they belonged.

Later, at home, Ayana relaxed with a shower, some chocolate, and a good movie. But she'd chosen a romantic drama and by the end, tears dripped from her nose and face. This was bad. If she'd remembered Justin, she would never have chosen that movie.

Justin had broken her heart, plain and simple.

She'd been so sure he'd propose, but in the end he'd dumped her. Just another marker in an endless spiral of bad relationships, but Justin had affected her more than she cared to admit. So she'd broken the cycle and signed up for police academy. Better to protect the public than continue making excuses for her deadbeat romantic partners.

To get her mind off of Justin, Ayana got off the couch and went into her home office. She wasn't allowed to take the official case files from the department but she'd gotten pretty good at finding

news clippings and information off the internet about cases that meant a lot to her. Usually cases that were unsolved.

Like the one right in front of her.

Tatiana Jefferson. Twenty-eight years old. Fragile and beautiful in a tired sort of way. She'd come into the department one rainy Sunday afternoon a few weeks ago, crying and saying that her lover kept watch over her like a hawk. Of course they'd gone to investigate - Ayana and her partner on the force - but there was no evidence to back up the woman's claims and she'd even dropped any complaints or charges she had against her lover once she was back home.

Nothing more had been said or done besides a couple drive-bys. Everything looked normal.

But the case had never left Ayana's mind.

Was Tatiana still controlled by her lover?

She should have been relaxing, but instead she opened the file. After all, work *was* relaxing to her. In a way.

After reading everything she'd been able to pull up on Tatiana and her lover, Ayana glanced at the clock. It was past midnight.

She'd found out everything she could for now so she set the file aside. Next morning she would look in the case file at the station and see if there was any new information or something she'd missed the first time.

As she flipped through the slim case file down at the station, Ayana remembered the last time she'd spoken with Tatiana. The woman had asked if Ayana had any advice about her handling her controlling lover and how she could escape should anything horrible happen.

Even now, several weeks later, anger rose up in her as she remembered Tatiana's fright. How had she let this go on for so long, unattended?

There was a CD in the file, one Ayana didn't remember seeing. When she flipped it over, there was a sticker on the front that said "TRANSCRIPT: DATE MARCH 28TH, 2004: INTERROGATION ROOM C: TATIANA JEFFERSON: DETECTIVE AYANA HARRIS".

So it was the recorded transcript of her conversation with Tatiana. She popped it into her computer. Maybe the refresher would give her some new insights into Tatiana's situation.

AYANA: How may I help you?

TATIANA: I thought when I got into a relationship with this man that it would be my last. I was wrong. At the beginning, it was good.

Great, even. But things got stranger and stranger the more time I spent with him.

Ayana transcribed the rest of the conversation and then found Tatiana's phone number in the file.

"Hello?" It was Tatiana's voice, still fresh in Ayana's memory from the recorded interrogation. Ayana gripped the phone, even smiled a little because at least Tatiana was still alive.

"Good afternoon, Ms. Jefferson," Ayana said. "This is Detective Ayana Harris. I was wondering if you could come out to my office. I'd like to see you again, make sure you're all right."

"I-I'll try," Tatiana said.

"Good. Would tomorrow afternoon work for you?"

There was a long pause. "I'll be there tomorrow, if I can," Tatiana said at last.

"Thank you. I look forward to seeing you then."

Chapter 3

Ayana organized the case files on her desk. Tatiana's was the one on top but she still looked through her other case files. Tatiana's might not be the most important. But the other files were a mix of petty thievery, smashed windows, and the like. She could focus on Tatiana's case with no guilt. After all, the woman was afraid her lover would do something violent if she made him angry.

The phone rang.

"Hello," she said.

"Hello, Harris. This is Assistant Chief Evans."

"Oh!" She straightened in her chair as if he could see her.

"I'd like you to come over to my office after you've finished whatever you're currently working on."

"I'll be there as soon as I'm finished my case reports."

"Thanks, Detective."

Fifteen minutes later, she knocked on Evans' office door and walked in.

"You asked to see me, sir?"

Evans smiled and gestured to a seat, the same one she'd sat in when she told him of her plan to capture Wilks. "Please have a seat." As she sat, he added, "Thanks for coming. The reason I asked you over here is because I wanted to thank you personally for all the work you did with the Wilks case. You handled that very well. Very professionally."

She forced herself not to flush. "Thank you, sir."

"And I also asked you here to speak about something more... personal."

"Sir?"

"Detective Harris, I understand that you deal with some very intense cases most of the time. But you never let those cases get to you and that's what I admire about you. I've never seen someone handle cases as well as you have done."

Was this flattery or the truth? His smile was warm, genuine, as he waited for her reply. So he had to be telling the truth, though she didn't think she was the best detective in the force.

"Well, I just put myself in the criminal's shoes and try to think as he or she would. I try to get inside their head, figure out what they'd do next."

"Not many do that," Evans said. "But it obviously works. Now, I understand you've taken on an old case. What's this one about? Why is it important to you?"

"I want to keep something awful from happening to a young woman before it's too late. I want to get her away from her controlling lover."

Evans nodded. "Good luck. And if you wouldn't mind, I'd like to hear more about the case when you've wrapped it up." He slid a paper across the desk toward her. "That's my personal number. You can call me anytime with questions or concerns."

She took the paper. "Thank you, sir. But aren't you going back to Virginia PD soon?"

"I'm helping with a backlog of cases right now," he said. "I might even ask for a permanent transfer. I like this station. The people, too."

He was looking right at her when he said it. There could be no mistaking his meaning. Assistant Chief Evans liked her? Ayana excused herself from the office as soon as possible, her mind racing. She wasn't sure if she liked him back. He was nice enough, but there was a smoothness about him that reminded her of Justin.

Her cell phone buzzed, distracting her from the issue. At least for the moment. It was Tatiana.

"Detective Harris," she said, her voice scratchy. "It's getting worse. I'm frightened."

"Okay, just stay calm. What happened?"

Ayana walked into the bullpen and sat at her desk, switching the cell phone to her other hand so she could take notes if needed.

"He's grown increasingly violent. He's never hit me - yet - but he just left the house, extremely angry, and I'm afraid he'll come back and do something to me. Please help me."

"All right," Ayana said. "I'll be there as soon as possible."

Chapter 4

She met with Willis and Harrington on the steps of the police station.

"We don't know what we'll find when we get to the Jefferson residence," Ayana said. "But you'll be my back-up officers in case something's gone wrong - which I hope it hasn't."

Willis and Harrington nodded. They took one vehicle while Ayana slid into her own car. They had the Jefferson address, but they stayed behind her all the way there like a proper escort.

Ayana called Tatiana as she drove. "I'm on my way," she said.

"Thank you," Tatiana almost sobbed. "Thank you so much."

They arrived at the Jefferson home ten minutes later.

Ayana knocked on the front door. There was a crash, the sound of a woman crying, and a shouted curse, definitely a male voice. Appearently Tatiana's partner had returned. Ayana steadied herself, hand resting near her handgun, as footsteps came closer and closer.

The partner flung the door open, a scowl on his face.

"I'm here to speak with Ms. Jefferson," Ayana said.

"Whaddya want with her?"

"We're here to make sure she's safe."

He muttered another curse. "She's fine."

"I'd prefer to see for myself."

"Got a warrant?" he said, arms crossed in front of his chest.

"No. But what I do have is probable cause, thanks to what I heard just before you opened the door." She stepped closer to the creep. "I suggest you let me in before I have Officers Willis and Harrington arrest you right here."

He finally stepped back, grumbling under his breath.

Ayana entered the house. The living room was to her right - that's where the crying came from - and she entered to find a lamp shattered on the floor and Tatiana sobbing, trying to clean up the mess. Bruises mottled her face and arms.

"Please help her," Ayana whispered to Harrington. She turned to the partner. "You're under arrest for domestic violence. Willis, take him down to the station."

Willis' clenched jaw and the glare he shot Tatiana's partner didn't bode well for the man.

"Harrington, you can go with Willis," Ayana said. "I'll handle things here."

As Harrington and Willis left with the partner, Ayana knelt down beside Tatiana - being careful not to hurt herself on the broken glass. "Ms. Jefferson, what happened?"

Tatiana stared at her for a moment and then hugged her, clinging onto Ayana like a drowning woman. Sobs shook Ayana, but they were not hers.

"Thank you," Tatiana said again and again. "Thank you. I broke the lamp and he-he got angry. Said he was going to kill me this time for sure." She gasped for breath against the tears. "Thank you. The neighbors must have heard all the times we fought, but they never did anything. Thank you for doing something."

Ayana swallowed down some tears of her own. She had to stay professional.

"It's my job," she said. "I'm glad that I could help you when you needed me. You don't have to worry about your partner anymore. There'll be charges pressed against him as well as a restraining order."

Tatiana nodded. "Thank you," she said again.

Ayana drove her to the hospital and, once she knew Tatiana would be given the best of care, headed back to the station to question Tatiana's partner. It wasn't strictly necessary, but like with Wilks, she wanted to know why he'd abused Tatiana. It was important to understand the mind of these criminals.

When she arrived at the station, she didn't go directly to the interrogation room. It was better to return to her desk and come up with a good line of questioning - maybe even jot down a few notes for the report she would have to make later on.

Just as she sat down at her desk, the phone rang.

"Hello, Ayana." It was Evans. "Just wondering how things are going with the Jefferson case."

"Ms. Jefferson's partner is in custody right now, sir."

"Exemplary work, Detective!" he exclaimed.

She glowed from the praise.

"Take a break for the rest of the day once you've wrapped things up here."

"Thank you, sir. I think I will."

After the call ended, she finished taking down notes on her observations and thoughts regarding the Jefferson case and then headed to the interrogation room. At times the endless cycle of hunting, arresting, and questioning got her even though she tried to fight against the depression.

At least the rest ahead of her sounded good.

She entered the interrogation room. Tatiana's partner sat there, smug and unrepentant, and familiar anger welled up inside her. How dare he be so calm about the whole thing! He'd committed such atrocities toward Tatiana.

"I guess you want to psycho-analyze me," he said. "Find out about my bad childhood and why I took it out on Tatiana."

Ayana set her chin. "I really don't want to know. I'm here to tell you that you've been charged with domestic abuse and if you somehow manage to dodge that, there's also a severe restraining order against you. You'll never see Tatiana again."

"Like I'd want to see her. The little-"

Ayana left the room before she could hear whatever names he called Tatiana.

She leaned against the wall and looked at the ceiling. She *had* planned to ask him questions, try to understand him better, but he was a louse that no one would ever understand. Why bother wasting her time?

She went home after that and tried to relax. It was almost impossible.

Evans called her again, too. It had to be true that he liked her or why else would he call her so often?

"I'm glad you're home now," he said. "Try to get some rest. You've been going for - what? Three days straight now?"

"Something like that." She put her phone on the speaker setting, too tired to even hold it anymore.

"Well, I'll let you get some rest. I was just wondering if you'd meet me for coffee tomorrow. I have something I'd like to discuss with you, the sooner the better."

"Why not at the station?"

He let out a long breath. "I'd like to talk with you, get to know you a little better. If we keep meeting at the station, people will start talking. Even if there's nothing to talk about."

"All right," she said through a yawn.

He gave her the address of the coffee shop he always went to and they said their goodbyes. Ayana turned off her phone, took a hot shower, and then crawled into bed. It had been a long day.

Morning came way too soon, in Ayana's opinion.

She threw on her clothes, gave her teeth a quick swipe with her toothbrush, and was about to head out the door when she remembered Evans' invitation last night. That's when she went back inside and chose her clothes a little more carefully, pinned her hair up, and took a couple breath mints.

There. That was better.

She got to the coffee shop earlier than their appointment but Evans was already there.

He waved her over. "I already ordered for you but if you don't like it, you can send it back."

She looked at the latte and the blueberry scone. "These are my favorites," she said. "How did you-?"

He grinned. "Let's just say that you're not the only detective here."

"You stalked my eating habits?" She didn't know whether to be amused or annoyed.

"Made some observations," he amended.

She couldn't help smiling herself, especially when she bit into the scone. The warm flakiness mixed with sweetness from the blueberries was perfection.

"So," he said. "You're probably wondering - yet again - why I asked you here, why I asked you to talk with me."

She nodded and took a sip of her latte.

"Well, to tell the truth, the reason has me confused as well."

"Oh?"

"I like you, Harris." He paused. "May I call you Ayana?"

"All right."

"Thank you. Like I said, I like you, Ayana. And not just as a fellow officer. You're the strongest woman I know."

The coffee turned bitter in her mouth. She didn't know what to think. He was handsome, yes. Talented and smart, yes. But she wasn't ready for a relationship with anyone and how could she have even caught his eye when she was so busy with her work all the time?

"Why?" she said.

"Why?"

"Why me? Why do you like me?"

He shrugged. "I can't tell you exactly how I came to admire you. But your dedication to your work, to protecting the helpless, captured my attention and I haven't been able to stop thinking about you." He gave a nervous laugh. Almost shy.

He looked at her, his gaze intense. "Would you consider dating me?"

Chapter 5

Ayana didn't know what to say.

"Chief Evans "Please. Call me Jonathan."

"Jonathan, I'll have to think about this."

He nodded. "You can take as long as you need. When you're ready to give me an answer, I'll be waiting."

Ayana sat at her desk, thinking.

In many ways, she didn't want to start another relationship with someone because of her past. But if she was going to turn Evans… Jonathan down, he needed to know the reason.

It would be rude to just refuse him and not give him a reason.

She'd never told anyone about her past, but it was time.

So she went down the hall to Jonathon's office. He welcomed her in warmly, probably hoping that she'd already decided to accept him. His eagerness was a shame, because after she told him about her past he probably wouldn't want to date her anymore.

"Jonathan, there's something you need to know about me before we take things any farther." She took a deep breath and forced herself to look him in the eye. "The reason I became a detective is because I had a boyfriend who verbally abused me and then raped me. I believed he loved me and that we'd get married in time, but that was all a lie."

She twisted her hands together. "When I found out he wouldn't marry me, I broke up with him. He snuck into my dorm room a few weeks later and raped me." She looked down at the ground. "I have a hard time trusting men now and I haven't been in a relationship since. And I-I don't feel like I'm ready for one now, either."

Jonathan's jaw twitched. "Thank you for explaining to me," he said. "You didn't have to, though. You could have just said 'no' and that would've been enough. I wouldn't have...pursued you, the way your ex did."

"I know." She managed a smile. "And I appreciate that about you."

"I would like an opportunity to show you that all men aren't horrible," he said. "I know you see the very worst abuse on the job, but not everyone in the world is like that." He shoved his hands in his pants' pockets. "Would you go out to dinner with?" he asked, holding up his hands to forestall her protest. "Not on a date! Just as friends. I promise."

He didn't want to take 'no' for an answer and while she didn't understand it, he was perhaps a person she could come to trust in the future. Maybe.

Didn't she owe it to herself to find out?

"One dinner," she said. "That's it."

He gave a relieved smile. "Thank you, Ayana."

They discussed when they would go out to eat and where - Jonathon was almost poetic in suggesting La Grotti, an Italian restaurant. Ayana agreed. She hardly ever ate out and Jonathan was obviously more experienced with the different eateries around Richmond.

"Saturday evening, then?" Jonathan said.

She nodded. "Sounds good to me."

"You can change your mind any time," Jonathan said. "I don't want you to be uncomfortable."

That was a relief. She didn't think she would change her mind about going out with Jonathan, now that she'd decided to go, but it was good to know that she could do so without him blowing up at her.

Chapter 6

It was Friday. Tomorrow she'd go out with Jonathon for dinner. Ayana didn't know whether to be excited or nervous - she was, she supposed, a combination of both.

She was writing her report on the Jefferson case when the phone rang. She wasn't surprised that it was Jonathon, but she was surprised by the urgency in his voice. It was so unlike the last time she'd spoken with him, which had to mean this was official business.

"Yes, Assistant Chief Evans?"

"There's a case downtown that needs your immediate attention," he said, his words rushing out. "A woman called, said her ex-husband has been beating on her pretty badly. I know you're the best one for the job."

"I'm on my way," she said, standing up.

"Good."

Ayana arrived at the up-scale residence downtown, Willis and Harrington coming in a separate vehicle behind her. She motioned for them to stay in the police car for the moment. A woman stood outside the house, her arms twisted around her waist. Even from this distance, Ayana could see the tears streaking her face and the bruises on her arms. Her hair was disheveled and tangled.

"I'm Detective Harris," she said. "I heard reports that your ex-husband has been beating you. Is that true?"

The woman nodded. "Yes. He doesn't want to accept that I left him."

Ayana set her jaw. The same old story, again and again. She felt a pang of sympathy for this woman. "What's your name?"

"Tamika. T-Tamika Summerton."

"Ms. Summerton-Tamika, if I may..."

Tamika nodded.

"Tamika, I deal with cases like yours quite often and I can assure you that you will never have to see your ex again unless you want to." Ayana put a hand on Tamika's arm, a quiet gesture of understanding. "We'll make sure he'll never have the opportunity to threaten or hurt you again."

Tamika blinked back tears. "Thank you, Detective. He's threatened my life before and I didn't know what to do."

"We'll find him," Ayana said. "And the more you help us find him, the sooner he'll be behind bars."

"I'll help in any way I can," Tamika said. A note of strength slipped into her voice with the words and as Ayana walked her back to the car, she felt her own strength returning. This was why she did what she did. To help helpless women regain control over their lives. To help the helpless in every way possible.

"Hey!"

Ayana turned. A man, his face contorted with anger, stomped towards them. Tamika trembled.

"Go to the squad car," Ayana said. "I'll take care of him."

As the man walked up, Willis came and stood beside her, a steady, reassuring presence. Though it would be foolish - though not inconceivable - for the ex to become physically violent with a police detective, she was still grateful for the support.

"Sir, you are under arrest," Ayana said when he was within speaking distance.

Willis stepped forward to cuff the man and the ex, threw a punch at Willis.

Ayana pulled out her handgun and trained it on the ex. "Not another move," she said.

Willis had been quick enough that the punch hadn't landed, but it was still unacceptable behavior. Willis cuffed the ex while Ayana covered him. Willis dragged the ex, away and Ayana got into the vehicle with Tamika.

"You'll be safe now," she said, though Tamika would probably have a hard time believing it for a while. Ayana knew all too well how hard it was to trust after such an abusive experience.

On Saturday night, Ayana couldn't decide between her strapless green evening gown or the purple sheath dress. She eventually went with the purple. It brought out her skin tones in the best way.

There was a knock on the door. Her pulse quickened and she checked her watch. Yes, it was about time for Jonathan to come and pick her up.

She opened the door.

"Ayana, you look..." He couldn't stop staring at her.

"So do you," she said, smiling. It felt odd, flirting when she hadn't done it in so long. But good, in a way.

They went downstairs together and Jonathon opened all the doors for her, just as a gentleman should. La Grotti was only a short drive away and since Jonathan had made a reservation, they were seated with menus in no time at all.

Ayana studied her menu and tried to keep from flushing with embarrassment. It was so long since she'd been on a date. What if she'd forgotten everything she once knew about making a good impression?

Not that this was really a date.

Even Jonathan had said so.

"I really do want to thank you for agreeing to have dinner with me," Jonathan said.

She smiled but she wasn't comfortable. Maybe it was the warmth of the room. "Thanks for taking me, Jonathan. And thank you for understanding why I don't really want to pursue a big relationship with someone right now." She glanced away, taking in the happy couples nestled in booths all around the restaurant. Someday, she wanted a relationship. When she could trust again.

"And I respect your reasons, Ayana. I really do. But speaking simply as another human being and not as someone who wants to date you-" He hesitated. "Closing your heart and spending the rest of your life alone just because some loser acted like a loser...it doesn't seem like a good idea." He took her hand and she let him. "I hope that someone will come and open your heart again and help you heal. I'm kinda hoping I'll be that person, if I'm being honest." He chuckled, a little shyly.

Ayana bit her lip. He was so kind. So helpful and caring.

Why was this so hard?

"I know you're probably wishing you'd never come," Jonathon said. "I don't want to make you feel like that. So I won't say anything more about it. You know my feelings and whatever you want to do about it, I'll respect that. I promise."

"Thank you, Jonathan."

Their orders came then - spaghetti and garlic bread for both of them. They ate and talked about small, unimportant things. Once, he even made her laugh. And that was a wonderful feeling.

When they reached Ayana's home, Jonathon parked the car but he didn't get out right away.

"Ayana, I know that you love your work. And you're good at it. But when was the last time you took a vacation?"

"I don't know." She shook her head. "I don't need one."

He sighed. "Promise me you'll let me know if you feel overworked. Let me help you if you ever want to get away for a few days."

"Thank you, Jonathan. I will."

"And-" He looked into her eyes. "May I give you a kiss before you go? Just on the cheek?"

He had been sweet. Probably nicer than she deserved.

"Yes," she said.

He leaned in and gave her a small kiss on the cheek. And after he opened the car door for her and escorted her up the steps to her home and after he'd gone, she could still feel the shadow of that kiss on her cheek.

Perhaps she could open her heart to Jonathan after all.

Chapter 7

"Briana, this is Ayana," Ayana said. "I need some advice."

She'd decided to call Briana - one of her best friends and one of the only people who knew what had happened with Justin - after the events of last night. The dinner, Jonathon's kindness, and especially the kiss had all left her confused. Who better to turn to than an old friend?

"What's up?" Briana said.

"Well, my boss took me out last night. La Grotti."

Briana whistled. "Nice place."

"I know. Anyway, I've told him most of the stuff about Justin and he was really sweet last night, letting me talk and not trying to push anything. And he kissed me when he dropped me off." Anaya shifted the phone from one ear to the other. "He wants me to think about a relationship between us. But I don't know what to do, especially after what happened with Justin."

Briana was silent for a moment. Then, "I'm not telling you to just get over the Justin thing. You know me better than that. But, Ayana, he sounds like a great guy. I definitely think you shouldn't brush him off, at least not right away."

"I know. And he told me to take some time off, some time for myself."

"Well, he's not wrong there. You know what I think you should do?"

"What?"

"Take a breather to really weigh your options. Ask yourself whether or not you could see your relationship with this Jonathon developing into something more. You owe that much to yourself."

"Thanks, Briana." Ayana smiled, though Briana couldn't see her.

They said goodbye and Ayana set her phone down on the table. Briana and Jonathon were right. A small break could help her approach all of this with a clearer mind.

She called Jonathan. Ordinarily, she'd speak with the Chief himself and ask for a few days off, but Jonathan was good friends with the Chief anyway and he'd been the one to suggest the break.

"Hey, Jonathan."

"Ayana! I was just thinking about you."

How did she respond to that? She didn't know, so she went ahead, "Jonathan, I've thought about what you said, about taking a break, and you're right. I've been pushing myself too hard. So I'm going to take you up on a few days' leave."

"That's great, Ayana. I'm glad."

"Me too. Talk to you later."

"Goodbye."

Less than a day in, and Ayana couldn't take it anymore.

She was so bored.

After getting out her laptop and clicking through old case files, hoping some loose end would jump out at her, she turned on the TV. Maybe someone needed her help right now. But there was nothing.

She ended up dozing off, even with the TV on, and when she woke up a couple hours later, she knew there had to be a change. She couldn't just sit around the apartment because that was boring and when she was bored she got stressed. Not a relaxing mini-vacation at all.

The coffee shop where she and Jonathon had met was open and she went in and ordered her usual latte. As she sipped it, her cellphone rang.

Jonathan?

But when she answered it, Briana's voice chirped in her ear.

"Just wanted to catch up," Briana said. "Your last call had me worried for you."

"Worried?"

"You were pretty stressed about everything. I could tell."

Ayana smiled. "Well, I'm doing better now. I told Jonathon I was taking a couple days off work. When I get back, I'll let him know what I've decided about our relationship. I'm actually just at The Roasted Bean, thinking some stuff through."

"I'm literally five minutes away," Briana said. "I could meet you there!"

"Sure," Ayana said. "I'd love to talk some more."

Ayana returned home. Her talk with Briana had been good. They hadn't spent much time to Jonathan or Justin or the fact that Ayana probably worked too hard. That was good. It was exhausting to talk about herself.

But Briana had helped her see some things more clearly and, even though it had been only a day away from work, she was ready to return to the station. And ready to give Jonathan an answer.

The station felt the same. Ayana scanned her computer for anything she might have missed, but new cases were thankfully low. She'd be able to catch up in no time.

Once she'd determined nothing needed her immediate attention, she headed for Jonathan's office. He welcomed her in, as he always did.

"How did you enjoy your day off?" he asked after she'd taken a seat.

"Well, to tell the truth, it was kind of boring." She laughed a little, but now wasn't the time for dodging the real issue. He needed to know her answer. He deserved to know her answer. "But I came to decision while away."

"Oh?" He leaned forward a little.

"You asked me to think about the possibility of a relationship with you," Ayana began. She let out a breath that would hopefully let out her nervousness as well. "And I've thought about it. I'm open to the possibility but I just don't know when I'll be able to fully trust anyone. Not just you - this isn't a personal thing, I promise. I have a hard time trusting anyone. But I'll let you know the moment I'm ready to take the next step."

Jonathon looked away, his jaw working. Was he disappointed? Heartbroken? Angry? She didn't know. But his voice was calm enough when he said, "Thanks for letting me know, Ayana. So we're just friends for now?"

She nodded. "Yes. I'm sorry...I wish it could be different."

"No. That's all right." He gave a brief smile. "I understand." He, too, took a deep breath and then riffled through the case files on his desk. "All of our personal business aside, I have a new case for you."

Ah. Work she could handle. "What is it?"

"A young woman recently reported that she'd been raped. She went to a party, got pretty high from something slipped into her drink, and then she was followed home and raped." He handed her the case file. "Considering your own history, if it's too personal for you, I completely understand."

She flipped through the file. "I've come to terms with my past," she said. "I just want to get justice for the women who've gone through the same thing. I'll take the case."

"Good."

Jonathan held out his hand. "Friends, remember?"

And they shook on it.

The victim's name was Sarah Hampton and Ayana put a call through to her. They needed to set a time and place to meet so she could learn more about the case and the woman herself.

"Hello?" It was a young woman's voice, nervous and unsure.

"Hello. This is Detective Harris of Richmond PD. I'd like to speak with Ms. Sarah Hampton."

"I'm Sarah."

"Ms. Hampton, I've received the report you gave. You said that you were raped in your home after a party. Is that correct?"

"Yes."

"Ms. Hampton, I will need to meet with you as soon as possible. Can you come down to the station this afternoon?"

"I'm too afraid to go anywhere," Sarah said. "Could you meet me here, at my home?"

"Yes, of course."

Sarah gave her address and Ayana promised to be there as soon as possible.

"I'm sorry if I inconvenienced you by having you drive out here," Sarah said when she met Ayana at the door.

"You don't have to apologize, Ms. Hampton.

I completely understand."

Ayana followed the young woman into the living room. There was a pot of coffee and some cookies on the coffee table, but Ayana didn't take in. She wasn't allowed to accept food or drinks on the job. If Sarah noticed, she didn't say anything.

"Now, please tell me everything you remember about the events surrounding the party and your attacker," Ayana said.

"I was invited to a party. It was going pretty good but I had one drink too many and the last one tasted weird, like a funny aftertaste, you know? It made me nauseous, so I decided to go home. It was only a couple blocks away." She looked away. "When I woke up, I was naked and bruised, so I went to the doctor. He confirmed everything."

Ayana clenched her jaw. For someone to take advantage of a defenseless young woman...the man had to be a monster.

"I'm going to find who did this to you," Ayana said. "He'll be put behind bars, I promise you." She tapped her pencil against her notepad. "Do you have any idea who could have done this? Tell me any suspicions you have - it could make everything go faster."

"There was a man at the party. He said...some things. Made some suggestions." Sarah bit her lip. "When I blew him off, he got pretty angry but I didn't see him after that. I thought he'd left the party."

"Do you have a name?"

"I think it was Douglas something." Sarah thought for a moment. "Douglas Wiggins. I think that's it."

"Thank you, Ms. Hampton. You've been a tremendous help." Ayana stood and so did Sarah. "We'll catch the culprit and I promise that he'll never be able to hurt you again."

Sarah smiled weakly. "Thank you, Detective. Thank you so much."

Chapter 8

Back at her desk, Ayana read through the information from Sarah's case. There was the case file, of course - still slim because the case was fresh - and the copious notes she'd taken down while Sarah talked.

She'd find this Douglas Wiggins and speak with him.

Well, probably do more than just speak. If the man was the rapist, he'd be arrested and put behind bars.

Elisa, one of the rookies, poked her head into the bullpen.

"Detective Harris?"

Ayana looked up. "Yes?"

"Officer Harrington just pulled a suspect in. I heard you mention his name in the dispatches so I thought you'd like to know."

"Who is it?"

"Douglas Wiggins."

Ayana sprang to her feet. "Where is he now?"

"Holding Cell B, I believe."

"Thanks," Ayana said. "I'll be there right away."

When she got to the interrogating room, she buzzed for Harrington to bring Wiggins in at once. She entered with the man. "Thanks, Harrington. Good work," she said.

Harrington nodded. She took a position in the corner of the room, customary procedure so that there could be another witness if the suspect made a confession and also for protection. Even if Wiggins was handcuffed to the table, something could still happen. Stranger things definitely had.

"Why am I here?" Wiggins demanded.

Ayana sat down facing him. "You're accused of drugging and raping a young woman."

"And what if I did?"

Ayana's jaw clenched. "You know what will happen."

He rolled his eyes. "You don't have proof."

"We have the testimony and the victim and grounds for a DNA test."

His expression shifted to one of shifty nervousness.

"I have rights."

"I'm not sure what 'rights' you're talking about, but we *will* take a DNA sample and we *will* find out if you're the rapist."

Wiggins gripped the edge of the table.

"It might be better to confess now," Ayana said. "Save yourself trouble. And if you confess willingly, it might go easier for you." Not that she wanted it to, but she wanted this over as soon as possible and the advantages for Wiggins weren't all that great.

His breaths came quick and shallow. "All right," he said. "All right, I did it. But I'm not sayin' it was rape and I'm not sayin' I drugged her." He looked from Ayana to Harrington. "You gotta believe me."

But Ayana had heard enough.

"She wanted it, believe me-" Wiggins began, but Ayana left the room. She didn't have to listen to his lies and his crudities. She spoke with the guard outside.

"Take him back to the cell, please."

She called Sarah and told her that Wiggins had been apprehended and that he'd confessed. But she didn't bother to relay Wiggins' protestations of innocence. They were useless at best and would upset Sarah at worst.

Footsteps approached her desk. It was Jonathon.

She ended the call with Sarah.

"Sir?"

"I heard you wrapped up the Hampton case."

"Yes." Ayana couldn't keep the smile off her face. Putting these criminals away was her vacation.

"Listen, I just dropped by to ask if you'd like to have dinner with me tomorrow."

"Sure," Ayana said. Maybe she was just riding the wave of adrenaline from Wiggins' capture and confession, but she actually wanted to go out with Jonathon.

"Great! Same place, same time?"

"That sounds good."

"Excellent. I have a surprise for you, too." He smiled.

After he'd left, she put her hands to her burning cheeks. When had she become so flustered in his presence? And what was the surprise he'd mentioned? Good thing tomorrow was so close - she didn't know if she could bear the suspense.

The food was delicious, just as it had been the last time. Ayana ordered the spaghetti again - she didn't like ordering something different just for the sake of, well, ordering something different. But Jonathon had the pizza.

"I guess you're wondering what the surprise is," Jonathan said.

"Well, I am kind of curious," Ayana admitted. She hadn't been able to stop thinking about it most of the morning and afternoon as she worked and then prepared for the dinner.

He cleared his throat. "Ayana, since the first moment I saw you, I liked you. And that feeling has only deepened every time we've spoken or worked together, and most recently when we had dinner together." He ran a hand through his short-cropped hair. "I don't know how to explain it, except to say that-that I'm in love with you. I want you to be part of my life and I want to be part of yours."

"What?" Ayana stared. "Are you serious?"

"I've never been more serious. And I'd never do anything to hurt you. I promise."

Ayana sat back. He loved her? How was it possible?

He reached into his jacket pocket, pulled out a tiny box. Was it-?

Inside, a diamond ring sparkled with all the fire it could pull from La Grotti's dim lighting. "Ayana, I want you to have this ring. You don't have to do anything right now, you don't have to accept me, but if you'll have me...I want to marry you."

He slipped the ring onto her finger as she sat there, shocked.

She didn't even know if she loved him, loved him enough to marry him.

"I-I don't know, Jonathan."

"Take as much time as you want. I mean it. I know that trust doesn't come easily for you and I'm not going to push you to make a decision. Just consider my proposal - please."

"I will. I will consider it, Jonathan." She leaned forward and this time it was she who kissed him. But only on the cheek.

Chapter 9

Ayana started awake.

A dream-

It had all been a dream-

But then she remembered. Everything flooded back when she looked at the ring on her finger. Jonathan had asked her to marry him and she'd put him off once again. Part of her wanted to make this leap of faith, but another part of her was terrified to do so.

She needed coffee and she needed to think.

Coffee in hand, she dialed Briana's number.

"Hey, Ayana!" Briana said, her voice perky as always. "How're you doing?"

"Hey. Well...I'm not sure. I've got another dilemma on my hands."

"Okay. What's got you rattled?"

Ayana took a deep breath. "The last time we talked, I really did what you told me. I opened my heart to new possibilities - at least, I thought I did. So, last night Jonathon took me to dinner again but this was completely different from last time."

"How so?"

"He asked me to marry him. And he gave me a ring."

"Oh my goodness!" Briana all but shouted. "Please tell me you said yes!"

Ayana took a sip of her coffee and steeled herself for Briana's reaction to the fact that she *hadn't* said 'yes'. "Well, I told him I needed time to think about it. But he understands! He knows what I've been through."

"Ayana" Briana went all serious. "If he loves you and you love him and he's willing to care for you - and willing to wait for you, no less - then why on earth wouldn't you say yes?" She blew out a long breath. "I mean, I get that you've been burned in the past but Jonathan sounds like a great guy. I think you should go for it."

Maybe Briana was right. Maybe she should put her past behind her and move on.

"All right. I'll think about it," Ayana said.

"Let me know what you decide. And let Jonathan know!"

"I will."

After the call ended, Anaya finished her coffee. She was needed at the station and would probably get there late anyway. As she set her mug in the sink, a bit of morning sun caught on the ring's diamond. It was a beautiful ring and a beautiful gem. Jonathan was very good to trust her with it even though she hadn't accepted him.

And, suddenly, she knew what she had to do.

"Ayana! I didn't expect to see you." Jonathan rose from his desk and came around the side of it. "Come in! Sit down."

"Thank you," she said. "Jonathan, I've come to a decision and you need to be the first to know."

He sat back down, but he was nervous. His hands fidgeted, couldn't seem to rest anywhere, and he busied himself with the documents on his desk. He didn't meet her eyes when he said, "Oh? And what have you decided?"

"I've decided-" She swallowed. Looked away herself.

"I've decided to accept your proposal, Jonathan."

He shot to his feet. "Really? That's-that's amazing! Thank you, Anaya. Thank you so much.

I promise you'll never regret it."

She was getting married. This was really happening.

Ayana hadn't slept much the night before, but it was a good kind of not sleeping. There were still issues to be worked out - office romances were never looked on with much approval and some people would assume she was a gold-digger for dating and marrying her boss. But she and Jonathan would work through it all. Together.

A knock came on the door.

She opened it to find a delivery man.

"Hello," he said. "I'm here to deliver this bouquet of roses to a Ms. Ayana Harris."

"I'm Ms. Harris."

"Here you go, Ms. Harris!" He handed the bouquet to her, velvety, rich red roses cushioned in a bed of tissue paper and gold confetti.

"Thank you," Ayana said. She put them in water first thing and then called Jonathon.

"I got the roses you sent. Thank you so much!"

"You're very welcome," he said. She could hear his smile even through the phone. "I hoped you'd enjoy them, even if they aren't as beautiful as you."

Ayana blushed. Good thing Jonathan couldn't see her right now. "Thanks for the compliment," she said, laughing a little. "Hey, do you want to meet for breakfast? If you're available, that is?"

"Sure," Jonathan said. "I'll come pick you up."

"I've heard about what happened to you at University," Jonathan said. "We don't ever need to talk about it unless you want to. But I was just wondering if you had any other worries that I could help with."

They sat at a tiny table for two, eating their danishes and sipping lattes. It was the most relaxed and happy Ayana had been for quite some time and she loved the feeling almost as much as she loved Jonathan.

She shrugged. "Mostly, I'm afraid of not being the best I can be. Not being good enough to help others in a bad situation."

Jonathon leaned forward. "Believe me, Ayana, you don't have to worry about that. I've seen your work as a detective and I can think of no one with more compassion than you. You care about everyone - even the criminals - and it's what made me fall in love with you in the first place."

She nibbled her danish, trying not to break down.

She was good enough?

She was kind enough?

"Thank you, Jonathan." Her voice caught.

"Are you okay?"

"Yeah." She sniffled. "I just haven't felt like this in a very long time."

"Like what?"

"Like-like I'm enough." She smiled. "Thank you for making me feel that way." So she had found him, then. The one man she could truly trust with her heart. "And thank you for helping me trust again. I-I love you, Jonathan."

His grin almost split his face. "And I love *you*, Ayana Harris."

When she got home from the station that night, she called Briana - something that was long overdue - and told her about accepting Jonathan's proposal and how Jonathon was truly the one.

"He sent me roses this morning and then we went out for breakfast. It was so wonderful! And I told him I loved him."

"Oh my goodness, that's amazing news, Ayana! I'm so happy for you! Have you decided on a wedding date? What kind of wedding dress are you going to wear? Who's your maid of honor?" Briana paused for a quick breath and then added, "Tell me everything!"

"Slow down, please." Ayana laughed. "We haven't decided on a date and I don't know what to do about my dress or how to plan a wedding or anything like that. Actually-" She dragged the word out for full dramatic effect. "I was wondering if you could help me with the wedding; I don't want to make a mistake."

"Of course I'll help!"

"And you're my maid of honor," Anaya added. "I wouldn't think of choosing anyone else."

"Thank you, Ayana! I'm so excited."

The next night, over dinner, she and Jonathon discussed wedding plans. It was all moving so fast, the wedding and the plans and everything. It was a little overwhelming. But good.

"I spoke with my friend, Briana, today. She was very excited for us."

Jonathan smiled. "And I spoke with my best friend, Alfonso. He's looking forward to the wedding as well."

"I'd love to meet him."

"I'm sure we'll all meet soon." Jonathan swiped across his phone's screen. "Do you have a possible date for the wedding yet?"

"I was thinking maybe the 20th of February. That would give us six months or so to plan. Unless you want a different date...?"

Jonathan shook his head. "No, that sounds perfect."

"All right, then. I'll start looking for possible venues - the earlier we book, the better."

Jonathan brought a case file to her the next day and laid it on her desk.

She looked up. "What's this?"

"A case with a unique twist. Kidnapping and rape."

It was an old story. Ayana raised an eyebrow. "What's the twist?"

"Apparently, a woman has kidnapped a man. She refuses to let him go until he confesses to raping her."

"What are their names and where has the woman taken the man?"

"The woman's name is Gardenia Banks. The kidnapped man is Harley Green and she claims that he manipulated her to get her alone and then raped her. She managed to grab his wallet and used that to find out where he lived. She kidnapped him the next day and is holding him hostage, saying she won't let him go until he confesses."

"And he hasn't?"

Jonathan shook his head.

Clever woman. But kidnapping was a crime just as rape was. They'd both have to face justice, though surely a judge would let Ms. Banks off easier than Green.

After Jonathan left, she studied the file. Ms. Banks was most likely holding Green in an empty warehouse at the center of the city.

Chapter 10

Ayana stood before Officers Peters, Washington, Willis, and Harrington.

"In a couple minutes we'll head to a warehouse where a Ms. Banks is holding suspect Harley Green. You'll be my back up. We need to bring both of them back to the station."

The officers nodded. They knew their work, just as she did. Ayana stepped out of the office and headed outside to her vehicle.

They spread out and searched the warehouse. The ceiling soared over Ayana's head, it was so high, and she kept her gun out.

Her radio crackled.

"This is Willis. We found them."

Faintly, she could hear Harrington shout, "Hold it, Ms. Banks! Put the stick down. You're under arrest!"

Ayana nodded. "Excellent work, Officer Willis."

She tried to brush away her disappointment. She should have been the one to speak with Ms. Banks and help her get through the next few minutes. But Willis and Harrington were good, capable officers. They'd get the job done.

She spoke briefly with Ms. Banks in one of the interrogation rooms, but there was little she had to do. The woman admitted everything freely. There was a genuine honesty and kindness about Ms. Banks and it made Ayana all the more angry that her kindness and goodness had been taken advantage of.

"Mr. Green won't even come near you anymore," she said. "And I'll make sure to speak with the judge on your behalf."

"Thank you," Ms. Banks said. "I appreciate it, Detective."

Then she moved into the next interrogation room.

The one where Harley Green waited.

"Hello, Harley. I'm Detective Harris." She sat down opposite him. "Do you know why you're under arrest?"

Harley spat on the floor. "No, *detective*, I don't. You should arrest that crazy woman for kidnapping and torturing me!"

"That woman is not crazy. She was hurt - by you - and the charges she's facing are nothing compared to what you're up against."

"Well, good luck proving anything." Harley crossed his arms over his chest and glared up at her, a mixture of defiance and hatred.

She would have laughed. "I've got news for you, Harley. Your DNA is in the system and it will prove that you raped Ms. Banks. Believe me, you've got nothing but prison ahead of you."

She met Jonathon in the hallway.

"What do you think?" he asked.

"He tried to turn the tables on Ms. Banks, make himself out to be the victim." Anaya shook her head. "In one sense, he is the victim but his crime is far worse, in my opinion."

Jonathon nodded. "I think so as well. What's your next move?"

"I'm going to speak with Ms. Banks one more time. She's the real victim here and it's my job to make sure she's all right."

"Good." He met her gaze. "I love you, Ayana."

She flushed and looked around. Had anyone heard?

"I love you too, Jonathan."

"Hello again, Ms. Banks. Thanks for waiting so patiently. I appreciate it."

"I just want this whole thing to be over," Ms. Banks said. She looked close to tears. "I want to try to feel safe again."

Ayana understood. Perhaps too well. "As far as I can make it so, everything will be all right. Mr. Green will never have a chance to hurt you again. He's going away for a very, very long time."

"I had to kidnap him!" Ms. Banks burst out. "I had to kidnap him and get a confession on tape. There are too many rape cases that are never solved and I needed justice." She rubbed her arm. "I didn't want him free to attack other women."

"I completely understand, Ms. Banks." Ayana hesitated. "You will be charged with abduction, I'm afraid, but I know the judge presiding over your case. He's more than fair and he'll bring everything into account. You'll still have to spend some time in jail, though."

Ms. Banks nodded. "You're just doing your job. I understand."

This was one of the hardest cases she'd ever worked on. Ms. Banks shouldn't have to spend any time in prison. In fact, Ayana wasn't sure she would have cared if the woman had killed Harley. But that, of course, was exactly the wrong sort of thought for a police detective to have. She shoved it away.

"I know you feel badly that Ms. Banks was charged at all," Jonathon said at dinner the next night. Ayana had told him some of her thoughts - just not all of them - hoping that he'd help her put things in proper perspective. "But even if it's a victim who takes the law into their own hands, we still have to uphold that law. Even as difficult as it might be."

"I know. I still can't help feeling that we should have let it go." Ayana took a sip of water. "But if we don't protect the law, then the law will protect no one."

"Exactly." Jonathan took a sip of water. "Now, how are wedding plans going?"

"Slowly, with the Banks case. I'm sure when Briana starts working on the wedding, things will speed up." Ayana smiled. Her friend was a force of nature. "And I'm wondering when we should announce our engagement at the station. I'm sure people are getting suspicious of the amount of time we spend together."

"We are surrounded by detectives, after all."

"Exactly!"

"We could tell them tomorrow."

"All right." Ayana took a sip of water to cover her nervousness. "And I'll bring some sort of refreshments in case people want to celebrate."

"Excellent!"

They finished their meal together, talking and laughing and discussing where their future would take them.

"I've found the perfect place to shop for my dress," Ayana said. "Blush on Berry Boutique. I'd definitely appreciate your help picking the perfect one."

Briana almost squealed into the phone. "Of course!"

After dinner with Jonathan, Ayana had returned home and realized that Jonathon's questions about the wedding had made her excited for it as well. So she'd stayed up late researching wedding dresses and boutiques and then called Briana. Briana was a night owl and, per the norm, was still awake when Ayana called.

"Of course I'll help you," Briana continued. "You're my best friend - how could I not?"

"Thanks, Briana. You're the best."

Ayana slipped the two bottles of alcohol-free apple cider into the station. Champagne would have been nice but not exactly appropriate for work hours. Jonathan came into the bullpen as she slipped the bottles into one of her desk drawers.

She could see the looks from the other detectives and officers in the room and her cheeks heated. But soon they'd understand.

"Hiding contraband, detective?" Jonathan asked, his voice teasing.

"As if I ever would."

He grinned. "I know, I know." He leaned a little closer. "I spoke with my friend, Alfonso, this morning and he really wants to meet you."

"And I want to meet him! Maybe we could all go out to dinner on Saturday? And I could bring Briana so we can all get to know each other."

"That would be perfect." Jonathon nodded. "I'll let Alfonso know."

Chapter 11

The morning passed so quickly that Ayana hadn't realized it was time to announce their engagement until Jonathon dropped by and rapped his knuckles on her desk. "It's time," he said.

She stood up and followed him into the center of the room.

"Excuse me, everyone," Ayana said. "Assistant

Chief Evans and I have an announcement to make."

"Yes," Jonathan said, pulling her to his side. "I've asked Detective Harris to be my wife and she said yes! We're officially engaged to be married this coming February."

"Congratulations!" someone in the back of the crowd said. And then there were flurries of congratulations from every corner, clapping, and cheering, and toasting Ayana and Jonathan.

She and Jonathan slipped away to his office when the attention became too overwhelming. "That was so

nerve-wracking!" Ayana exclaimed. Her legs still trembled underneath her.

"I was nervous, too," Jonathan said. Then he grinned. "But now everyone knows." He gazed into her eyes. "I can't wait for the wedding, my darling."

"Me neither."

Amanda Harrington stopped Ayana on her way back to her desk.

"Congratulations on your engagement, detective," she said, a smile widening her face. "I saw the look on Evans' face when he announced it; he really loves you."

"Thanks, Amanda." Ayana rested a hand on the officer's arm. "We're so happy together."

When she got home from work, she called Briana and told her about announcing the engagement and that she and Jonathon wanted to take Briana and Alfonso out to dinner. Her friend was enthusiastic about the idea and before Ayana ended the call, everything got settled.

She ended up calling Briana back after flipping through some bridal magazines. On one page, there was the picture of a gorgeous dress, one with an Empire waist and slender shoulder straps. It was perfect.

"Hey, what's up?" Briana said.

"Sorry to bother you again, but I think I've found the perfect wedding dress."

"Ooh, really?"

"Yes. Can we meet tomorrow to look it over?"

"Sure!"

The next day was Saturday, the day that Briana and Alfonso would get a chance to meet each other and, at the last minute, Ayana called Officer Harrington as well. They didn't know each other especially well, but she'd always admired the woman's grit and determination and with her opening her heart again to romance, she needed to open it to more friendships as well.

"Detective Harris?"

"Yes, hi. I want to invite you to dinner with me and Jonathon and a couple of our friends. It would be great if you could join us. Honestly."

Silence from the other end.

"And there's something I'd like to ask you when you come," Ayana added, as if Amanda had already agreed. "Please come."

"Oh, all right. What time?"

"7:30, at Cielito Lindo - the Mexican restaurant downtown."

"Yes, I know where that is. Thanks for the invite, detective."

"No problem."

When Jonathan picked her up, he handed her yet another bouquet of roses.

"I love you so much, Ayana," he said as he handed her the flowers. "Nothing will ever change that."

"Oh my goodness, thank you, Jonathan. They're beautiful." She smiled up at him. "I'll never stop loving you either. I know it."

"Shall we go?"

She nodded. "Let's do this."

It usually took about twenty minutes to get the restaurant but bad traffic held them up and when they arrived, Briana and Alfonso were already seated and talking with each other.

"Hello!" Ayana exclaimed and Briana gave her a bone-crushing hug. Briana was always like that.

"I'm so happy to be here," Briana whispered in her ear. She stepped away, allowing Ayana to tug her dress free of wrinkles again and prepare to meet Alfonso.

"Ayana, this is my friend, Alfonso Rivera."

She shook hands with Alfonso, a rather thin, rather tall Hispanic man. His eyes lit up with interest and he smiled. "Pleased to meet you, Alfonso." Then she turned back to Jonathan. "And please allow me to introduce my friend, Briana Bell."

Jonathan shook Briana's hand and then they all sat down. There was still no sign of Amanda, but surely she'd arrive. Ayana looked around the restaurant and jumped when Jonathan placed a hand on her arm.

"Ayana, are you looking for someone?"

"Oh, sorry, I forgot to tell you that I invited another friend from work. Amanda Harrington. And she's late."

But even as she said that, the door opened and Amanda walked in.

She sat down, introductions were made all over again, and then Jonathan rose.

"Thank you all for coming. I'd like to say something to Ayana, if I may." He looked around, as did Ayana. Warmth crept into her face as he went on. "Ayana, from the first moment I saw you and realized how dedicated and compassionate you were, I fell in love with you. There's no other woman for me and there never will be. I can't wait to spend the rest of my life with you."

Briana sighed dreamily, Alfonso slapped Jonathan on the back, and Amanda smiled. She seemed to finally relax.

Ayana turned to her. "Amanda, the reason I invited you here was to ask you for a favor that I hope you'll accept. I'd like you to be one of my bridesmaids. Please."

Amanda blinked. Then, "Of course I will if you want me to. But why?"

"I've always appreciated the work you've done and I think we could be really good friends. But please don't feel like you have to accept if you don't want to."

"No, I want to," Amanda said, a smile crossing her face. "Thank you."

"Thank *you*." Ayana grinned. "Now who wants some drinks?"

Chapter 12

Jonathan dropped her off at her house. "Ayana, darling," he said, "I hope that you enjoyed yourself tonight." He gazed down at her and, not for the first time, Ayana flushed under his gaze.

"Yes, I did." Ayana smiled. "I think Alfonso and Briana and Amanda did, too. I'm so glad she agreed to become my bridesmaid."

"I think she was surprised that you asked her," Jonathan said.

Ayana nodded. "We haven't spoken too much, beyond work-related business, but I've always wished that we could be better friends and besides Briana, I wouldn't have any other attendants at the wedding." She tucked a strand of hair behind her ear. "Not that I asked her just because I want another attendant!"

"I know." Jonathan smiled. "And Ayana, I want you to know that everything I said tonight about loving you and that you're the only woman for me...I won't change my mind. I meant every word."

Now it was her turn to say, "I know. And I feel the same about you."

"I promise to make you the happiest woman on earth, darling."

"And I promise to make *you* the happiest man."

After that, no more words were needed.

A few days passed, a bustle of work and pre-wedding jitters, and Ayana had all but forgotten about dress shopping until Briana called her the following Saturday.

"Hey, friend," Briana said. "You know what we're going to do today?"

"No idea." Ayana grinned anyway. Briana's voice held the promise of an exciting surprise.

"We're going to Blush on Berry Boutique to get you fitted for a wedding dress. Maybe even buy one right away if we're lucky and it fits. Which it should," Briana added. "You've got the most perfect figure."

"Sure," Ayana said, hoping her sarcasm translated through the phone.

"I'm serious. But anyway, meet you there in an hour?"

"Fine." She had nothing better to do and the wedding was coming up faster than she'd really expected.

When the call ended, before she got ready to go out, she gave Amanda a call. She was off work as well - their schedules usually coincided pretty well. Since Amanda was a bridesmaid, it only made sense for her to come along. After all, they'd probably get the bridesmaids' dresses and accessories at Blush on Berry as well.

"Hello?" Amanda said.

"Hello, Amanda. This is Ayana. I'm heading over to Blush on Berry Boutique in a few minutes to buy a wedding dress and I wondered if you'd like to come as well. I'll probably get the bridesmaids' dresses from the same place."

"All right," Amanda said. "I'll get there when I can - it might be a couple hours, though."

"That's fine. I'm sure Briana won't want to leave for at least five." Ayana laughed. "See you then."

As it turned out, they were all a little late getting to the Boutique and so Amanda arrived at almost the same time Ayana and Briana did. Even though the prospect of shopping for clothes didn't excite Ayana as much as it did Briana, it was necessary and the goal was to have fun together - not just shop. (Though to Briana, the two were interchangeable.)

"How does this one look?" Briana said, holding up a sheath wedding dress with lace covering the entire gown.

Ayana shrugged. She didn't like it, but Briana obviously did. She'd probably have to try it on.

"Hey, is everything okay?" Briana asked in a hushed voice. Amanda had wandered off to look at the different white shoes available.

"Yes, of course." Ayana smiled. "It's just that I haven't shopped for so long and the selection is pretty exhausting. It's hard to know exactly what I want." The image of the dress from the magazine still spoke to her, but the chances of find it - or one similar - were slim.

"You don't like this dress, right?"

"Well…"

"It's fine! I'll keep looking."

While Briana dived back into the clouds of fluffy white dresses, Ayana joined Amanda at the shoe section. She might as well pick up a new pair - somehow her tactical boots didn't strike her as appropriate wedding wear. She was just turning over a satin open-toed heel to check the price when someone tapped her on the shoulder.

"I found it!" Briana squealed and held out a dress, still on its hanger.

Ayana gasped. It was The Dress. Spaghetti straps and an elegant Empire waistline. It looked just as perfect up close. "How on earth did you find it?"

"I showed a saleswoman the picture you sent me."

Ayana almost rolled her eyes. Of course. How simple.

"I'll try it on right now."

The dress needed some minimal alterations so Ayana didn't leave with her dress, but they'd found gowns for both Briana and Amanda, along with shoes for all three and hair accessories so Ayana was satisfied. Briana had made everything move along so much more smoothly.

All that shopping had made her hungry so she suggested lunch together - her treat. "It's the least I can do for all your help," she said. Amanda had proved invaluable in figuring out the best deals and prices. And Briana had found the dress, of course. "You've both helped me so much."

"It's our pleasure," Amanda said, a smile breaking through her normally serious face. "And I had fun."

"So did I!" Briana exclaimed. "You're going to be an awesome bride."

Her cellphone rang. "Excuse me for a minute." She had a suspicion of who was calling and when she looked at the number, she was right. Jonathan. A smile spread over her face and Briana giggled.

"Hello," she said.

"Good afternoon, darling," Jonathan said. "How are you doing?"

"Great. I've been wedding dress shopping with Briana and Amanda."

"What a coincidence! Alfonso and I have been shopping for our tuxedos. We've had a good time." Jonathan paused. "I can't wait for our wedding."

"Me either. I'm glad you and Alfonso had a good time."

"Well, I'll let you get back to your friends. I love you, Ayana."

She was intensely aware of Briana - and probably Amanda - listening in to every word. But she still said it back to him. "I love you too, Jonathan."

Now that the wedding was coming ever closer and the preparations took up more of her time, Ayana wondered if it might be better to take time off of work and return after the wedding. There were pros and cons to both options and she ended up going into Jonathon's office. He'd provide some fresh perspective and he was still her boss, after all.

"Jonathan, with the wedding coming up so soon, do you think I should take on any more cases right now?"

He thought for a moment. "I think that would be a good idea. You've probably gathered quite a few vacation days throughout your time here, knowing how you hate taking time off." He winked. He always wanted her to take time off, to not overwork herself. Well, now he was getting his wish. "But I'll support you, whatever you decide."

And that was what she loved about him. Well, one of many things.

"I think I will take time off," she said. "I need to focus on this wedding."

But at the same time, she could only take this time off because there were no pressing cases. If one came up, she would have to take it. She wouldn't be able to help herself.

Chapter 13

The pieces of art in the museum took her breath away but nothing was as wonderful as Jonathan's presence beside her. She loved him more and more each day.

"Thank you so much for arranging this," Ayana said as they exited the museum. "It was a good break from all the wedding planning."

"You're more than welcome," Jonathan said, smiling down at her.

They went back to their respective apartments and changed into something a little more formal than their 'walking around the museum' clothes in anticipation for dinner out that night. While Ayana toweled her hair dry after a quick shower, she gave Briana a call and told her about how wonderfully the day had gone.

"That's great to hear," Briana said. "See, I knew I was right when I told you to accept Jonathan's proposal."

Ayana grinned. "Yes, you were."

"I'm just worried, Jonathan," Ayana admitted over dinner. She'd dressed up more than usual because she had to tell him something that had weighed on her heart for a few days now. She'd hidden it from everyone - even herself - but it demanded her attention, *their* attention no

He frowned in concern, his eyebrows quirking upwards. "About what, darling?"

She played with her napkin, plucking at a loose thread in the weave. "I've closed myself off from love for so long that I worry I'll be able to love you the way I should. I'm worried that I won't be the best wife you could have."

Jonathan shook his head. "You're the wife I want. And, believe me, there's more than enough love in my heart for both of us. Please don't worry about trying to be the best wife; I'll always love you, the way that you are."

She laughed a little. "I guess I'd still be working like crazy if you hadn't come along. So that's progress, anyway."

"Exactly! You'll keep me focused and I'll help you not work too hard."

"That sounds perfect," Ayana said. And she meant it.

The week away had ended all too soon and now it was time to return to work. A part of her wished that she could spend more time away from the station, away from the cases that demanded her attention. But there was a stronger, more insistent part that knew she had to return. Detective work was her first love and already she felt guilty over spending so much time away from people who might need her.

She got to the station on time and saw Amanda on her way in.

"Hey, Amanda," she said.

Amanda looked up and smiled from where she stood at the front desk, handing some files over to the desk sergeant. But Ayana didn't stop to say anything more. It was best to plunge right into her duties.

A short stack of case files sat in the center of her desk, waiting for her attention. She sat down, shrugging off her coat as she did so, and slid the first file off the stack.

Domestic abuse, again. Another husband abusing his wife and the wife asking for help out of the relationship. Some neighbors had called, reporting a possible altercation. It might have already been cleared up but she'd need to make sure. The woman's name was Ambra Smith, her house number listed beside her name.

Ayana picked up the phone and punched the number in.

"Good morning? Who is this?" a woman's voice asked.

"This is Detective Ayana Harris. Am I speaking with Mrs. Smith?"

"Yes, that's me."

"I'm sorry for calling so early, but I wanted to see how you were doing. I've got your file right in front of me. I'm going to send an escort to bring you back here and then we can figure out what to do about your husband."

"Thank you," Mrs. Smith said. "There were some officers here but they couldn't prove anything. But I'll come as soon as you send the escort."

An hour later, Ayana looked up to see a young woman approach her desk.

"Detective...Harris?"

"Yes."

"I'm Ambra Smith." The woman held out her hand. She was clear-eyed and straightforward, no visible signs of abuse on her arms or face. But Ayana didn't doubt her story for a moment.

"Hello, Mrs. Smith." Ayana pulled a chair over. "Please have a seat. Tell me everything about your husband."

"He's abused me for years and years. I've tried to get away but he's always found me."

"What made you decide to come to us now, after all these years."

Mrs. Smith looked away, blinked back tears. "I'm pregnant. And I didn't want to risk my husband hurting the baby."

Ayana sat back. "I understand. I'd like a doctor to examine you and then we'll take the appropriate next steps toward making sure that your husband never sees you again."

"Thank you." Mrs. Smith nodded. "I've been praying for this nightmare to end." And then her tears did fall. Ayana leaned forward and handed her a tissue.

"You'll be all right, Mrs. Smith. I promise." Ayana rubbed the woman's back until her sobs quieted. "I'm going to have a couple officers escort you to the hospital and I'll take care of everything on this end, okay?"

Mrs. Smith nodded. "Okay."

When the doctor's report came back that Mrs. Smith had indeed been abused, Ayana sent Amanda and Willis to apprehend Mr. Smith - that is, if he were still in the vicinity. Amanda updated her when they returned, the belligerent husband in tow.

"He told us that a piece of paper wasn't going to keep him from his wife. Told us that he'd do what he pleased." Amanda shook her head, a wry smile twisting her lips. "He's making it easier and easier."

Ayana nodded. "Sounds like it."

She placed a call to Mrs. Smith's cellphone. "Hello? Mrs. Smith? This is Detective Harris. We have your husband in custody and he'll be going up before the family court soon. We should get that restraining order in no time."

"Thank you, Detective! Thank you so much."

"I'm just doing my job, Mrs. Smith." And as she said the words, Ayana realized just how much she'd missed this. Not the accounts of abuse, but helping those in need. It was what she was meant to do.

Chapter 14

Ayana had only slept for a short time when she woke up, her mind in a whirl. The wedding was only a few months away and there was still so much to do.

Would her wedding dress be finished on time?

Would the decorations be what she wanted?

The wedding preparations never stopped, it seemed.

She called Briana to get her input over all the controlled chaos that the next several weeks promised to bring.

"Hey, what's up?" Briana said.

"I can't sleep, Briana. I'm worried about the wedding. It's all I can think about! We're almost at Christmas and the wedding is in February."

"Okay, okay." Briana paused. "You don't have to be worried about anything. Wedding prep is going great. Jonathan loves you a lot and that's all that matters. And you have me to help you, just like I've been doing."

Ayana blew out a deep breath. "You're right."

"And nothing's going to change our friendship, not even you getting married, right?"

"Of course not. You're like a sister to me."

"And you are to me. And everyone's behind you, supporting you. Trust me."

Ayana smiled. "I'll try to remember that. And I think you and I should get together to take care of any last minute details."

"Sounds good! Now get some sleep, friend. You have a busy day tomorrow, right?"

"Yes." Wedding preparations and work.

After her usual breakfast of hot coffee - and nothing else - Ayana headed into work the next morning. But there were no active cases on her desk - either the city was calmer than it had ever been or Jonathan was fielding out cases she normally would have taken. As long as she wasn't essential and no one else was being overworked, she was okay with that. It gave her time to catch up on paperwork.

But she made a mental note to ask Jonathan about her case load - or lack thereof - at dinner that evening.

As she worked over the backlog of case reports and filing, her mind wandered to thoughts of the wedding. Spending the rest of her life with Jonathan, the two of them getting to know the other better every day...it sounded like a wonderful dream. A dream close to completion.

Dinner with Jonathan was wonderful. When she asked him about available cases, he confirmed what she'd suspected: he was giving her cases to other detectives so she could focus on the wedding.

"Well, I'm going to do double work when we get back from the honeymoon," she warned, smiling. "I can't keep back from detective work, not when it's been my life for so long."

"Whatever you want, darling. All I want is to see you happy. You're so serious all the time," Jonathan said with a grin.

"I am happy, Jonathan."

And it was all because of him. In some ways, she could still hardly believe that such a handsome, successful guy like Jonathan would actually love her and want to be with her. But it was true. If she told Briana those thoughts, her friend would yell at her for thinking she was unworthy. And Briana would be right, she had to admit.

She deserved some happiness.

"I thought we could host a small Christmas party for friends and family," Ayana said. "Christmas Eve is only a couple days away and I think it would be fun."

Jonathan frowned. "Are you sure you can handle the wedding and a Christmas party?"

"Yes. Briana has been such a huge help with coordinating the caterers, the location, and the clothes. She's actually left me very little to do."

"All right, then. A Christmas party sounds good." Jonathan took a bite of his mashed potatoes. "If you need my help with anything, let me know."
"I will."

Even though she had to plan it in only a couple days, the Christmas party was a success. It was a tiny gathering of her and Jonathan's closest family and friends - friends like Briana and Amanda and Alfonso - and was held at Ayana's apartment. She wore a festive red dress that almost reached the floor. It went well with Jonathan's dark blue suit as she stood beside him, greeting the guests.

"Thank you for being here with us and celebrating the season," Jonathan said. "We appreciate it."
There were smiles and clapping, raised glasses and laughter.
It was an amazing party.

After it was all over, Jonathan pulled Ayana aside and handed her a small box.

"What is it?" she asked. "You already gave me a ring, remember?"

He laughed. "Open it."

She did. Inside the box gleamed a silver necklace. Hanging from the chain was a silver circle embedded with diamonds; engraved on the circle were the words "To Ayana, my forever love".

"Oh, Jonathon." Tears pricked her eyes as she looked up at him. "Thank you."

"You deserve it, darling. And so much more."

"I love you so much, Jonathon. You've made me so happy."

After that, nothing more needed to be said.

The days and weeks sped away, as they tend to do when people are as much in love as Ayana and Jonathan. At least, that's how it felt to Ayana when she woke up the morning of her wedding. It had come so quickly - and she was happy. Soon she and Jonathan would be together, always.

The rehearsal dinner last night had been beautiful. Jonathan had made one of his wonderful speeches, the rehearsal itself had gone well, and they'd all had a delicious dinner. If it was a true preview of what the wedding would be like, she had nothing to worry about.

She slipped out of bed and, as she brushed her hair, the phone rang.

It was Jonathan.

"Hello, darling. How are you doing? Today's the day!"

"I never thought this day would come," Ayana said. "But I'm excited. And a little nervous. I don't want anything to go wrong."

"As long as we get married, nothing else matters. That's how I feel about it."

"You're right." She smiled and set the brush down.

The doorbell rang. "Jonathan, I think Amanda and Briana are here - I'd better go."

"All right, darling. We'll see each other soon."

"Love you."

"I love you, too."

She left the bathroom and answered the door.

"Good morning, bride to be!" Briana squealed as she hugged Ayana. Amanda also greeted her, though a little more calmly.

"Good morning. Now, do I get dressed here or at the church?"

"Here!" Briana said. "It's a gorgeous day outside, for February. There isn't any rain or snow to ruin the lace or anything."

"Well, I'll need some help getting into it."

"Then let's get going! There's no time to waste."

Ayana peaked around the door that blocked her view of the sanctuary until it was time for her to walk down the aisle. She didn't have anyone to walk her down - all her family was still in the Sudan. But as long as she married Jonathan, it didn't matter how she got to the altar.

Amanda and Briana had already reached the front of the church. Any moment now…

The opening notes of Celine Dion's 'Because You Loved Me' echoed through the sanctuary. That was her cue.

Ayana took a deep breath.

Jonathan looked so handsome, standing at the altar. That was the first thing she thought when she entered the sanctuary. She was really doing this. Getting married to the man she loved.

It was a dream come true, a dream she thought would stay a dream for so long.

She reached the front of the church and took Jonathan's hand.

For better, for worse, she was doing this.

The ceremony proceeded smoothly, the customary readings, questions and answers, and so on. But the moment she'd been waiting for was when the priest indicated it was time for them to read out the vows they had written for each other.

"Jonathan, you made read your vows to Ayana."

Jonathan cleared his throat. She could see the emotions in his face. It prompted tears from her as well, though she blinked them away. Now wasn't the time to break down in tears, even if they were happy tears.

"Ayana, my sweetheart, my love...hold my hand and I will take you as my wife down this road before us. We will go arm in arm, with hearts aflame for each other. We will teach each other and learn how to love forever and ever."

Ayana blinked back some more tears.

"Thank you," she mouthed to Jonathan. His vows had been beautiful.

"Ayana, you may say your vows to Jonathan."

She took a moment to compose herself, and then spoke. "Jonathan, you know me better than anyone else in this world and, somehow, you still manage to love me. You are my best friend. You are my strength, my one true love. There's a part of me today that cannot believe that I am the one who holds your hand and heart. My own heart is forever yours."

Jonathan's eyes overflowed with love and gratitude. She could stare into those eyes all day. But there was still the exchange of rings.

"Do you, Jonathan Evans, take Ayana Harris to be your wife? To have and to hold, love and protect all the days of your life?"

"I do." Jonathan's voice was choked with emotion. He slid the wedding ring onto her finger.

"And do you, Ayana Harris, take Jonathan Evans to be your husband? To love, honor, protect, and cherish all the days of your life?"

She smiled. "I do." She took Jonathan's hand in hers. It was solid and warm. The ring fit perfectly.

"Then I now pronounce you husband and wife! You may kiss the bride."

Jonathan bent down and he kissed her like she'd never been kissed before.

"Everything you need, your courage, strength, compassion and love; everything you need is already in you."

About the Author:

Acai Louis Kuol Arop was born in Khartoum Sudan in 1981. She lives in Edmonton Alberta with her two children Alek and Mathiang. Writing has always been a part of her life, her day is not complete without putting pen to paper. Her main inspiration is her father Louis Kuol Arop, a retired Journalist, she remains grateful to her family in having faith in her talents as an author.

"You have within you
right now everything you need
to deal with whatsoever
the world can throw
at you."

This is to all women.

We Fall, we rise
We make mistakes, we learn
We get hurt, We bounce back
We are not PERFECT, we are human
We have confidence, we have faith
We will continue putting one foot in front
of the other and keep moving forward
That's what we Strong women Do!!
Please Never Give UP!!

Made in the USA
Columbia, SC
11 July 2020